Unicorn Prince

Zanna Davidson

Illustrated by Barbara Bongini

Meet the Ponies
Puck
Holly
Bluebell
Pony Queen
Princess Rosabel

Spray
Unicorn Prince
Izagard
Shadow

Fairy Pony Island

Lake of Gilded Lilies

Dark Forest

Tangled Forest

Unicorn Prince's Palace

Enchanted Wood

Dancing Waterfall

Pony Magic School

Magic Pony Pools

Sunlit Sea

Woody Glade

High Mountains

Izagard's House

Rainbow Mountain

Everlasting Rainbow

Summer Palace

Forever Flower Meadow

Rainbow Shore

Butterfly Valley

Silver Stream

Singing River

Meadows

N

W

E

S

Entrance from the Great Oak

Contents

Chapter One

"Goodnight, Holly," said Great-Aunt May, peering round the doorway of her attic bedroom. "Sweet dreams."

"Goodnight," Holly replied, smiling into the darkness. She listened to her aunt padding downstairs, then slipped out of bed and tiptoed as quietly as she could to her window. *Please let the moon be out,* thought Holly. She drew back the curtains, and as she did so, saw the moon shining out from behind a passing cloud. A moment later, a shaft of moonlight streamed down into her great-aunt's garden, lighting up a path to the old oak tree.

Holly turned and silently slipped down the stairs, through the cottage door and out into the garden. It was time to visit Pony Island again.

Holly was having her best summer holidays ever. At the bottom of her great-aunt's garden was a magical world full of fairy ponies, hidden inside an old oak tree.

And ever since she'd rescued Puck, the fairy pony, Holly was the only human allowed to visit their secret island!

She glanced around to make sure no one was watching, then she reached into her pocket and pulled out a tiny bag of magic dust that the Pony Queen had given her.

A few sprinkles later and she was fairy-sized – small enough to enter the hidden tunnel in the tree. But first she had to whisper the words of the spell:

"Let me pass into the magic tree,
Where fairy ponies fly wild and free.
Show me the trail of sparkling light,
To Pony Island, shining bright."

As soon as the last words of the spell left her lips, Holly saw a shining pathway ahead of her. She rang the tiny bell she always wore around her neck, then ran forward, her fairy-light feet barely making a sound on the smooth oak floor. Her heart fluttered with excitement. At the end of the tunnel, Puck, her best friend on Pony Island, would be waiting for her – he always came as soon as he heard the bell.

She turned a corner and saw a glimpse of Pony Island. With a new burst of speed, she raced down the last stretch of the tunnel and emerged into a sunlit meadow. A fresh summer breeze wafted over the long grasses, which brushed and tickled against her legs. For a moment Holly could only gaze at the view – a flower-filled valley running down to a sparkling river, and beyond that, a line of gently sloping hills, lush and green beneath a clear blue sky. Bees buzzed around her and butterflies flitted from flower to flower, but there was no sign of Puck anywhere. *Why hasn't he come?* thought Holly, filled with disappointment.

"Hello!" came a voice from above, followed by a mischievous chuckle as Holly jumped.

Holly looked up to see Puck hovering in the air, fluttering his butterfly wings, his glossy roan coat gleaming in the sunlight. "You should always remember to look up in Pony Island," he said with a grin, before swooping down to land beside her.

"And," he went on, full of excitement, "I've got another surprise for you." He bent down and lifted the flap of the basket he was carrying around his neck. Holly peered inside.

"Wow!" she said, glancing up to see Puck's eyes twinkling with merriment. "That's the most delicious picnic I've ever seen."

"I know!" said Puck proudly.

Holly laughed as she swung herself onto Puck's back. "Then what are we waiting for?" she said. "Let's fly!"

Puck fluttered his wings and the next moment they were rising up and up, over the waving grasses and nodding flowers, until they were flying high above the treetops. Holly wrapped her arms around Puck's neck and closed her eyes for a moment, letting the breeze wash over her, loving the feel of the wind in her hair.

"So what have we got in our picnic?" she asked dreamily.

"Berry cakes and rainbow drops and orange blossom icicle pops," said Puck. "We've even got some honeydew juice."

"Is that from Bluebell?" asked Holly, smiling at the thought of Puck's mother.

Puck nodded. "She put it in as a special treat for you."

As Puck chatted about the picnic, Holly gazed down at Pony Island. Puck swept out from a woody glade to soar above the Magic Pony Pools, a sparkling lake where all the fairy ponies went to wash and play. Soon, they were following the bend of the Singing

River, and Holly cupped her ear to hear its music; beautiful, lilting notes that rose from the water like birdsong.

"Here's our picnic spot," Puck said at last, twirling down to the ground by the banks of the river. "I found it with my friend, Dandelion."

"It's perfect," said Holly, taking in the bulrushes and irises crowding the riverbank, and the thick, springy grass that carpeted the ground like velvet.

They laid out the picnic together, but Holly couldn't stop gazing at the view. She loved visiting new places on Pony Island, knowing there was always a magical surprise around the corner. "What's that wood over there?" she asked, pointing to the other side of the meadow.

"That's the Enchanted Wood," Puck explained. "It's where the unicorns live."

"Unicorns!" Holly gasped in excitement. "I didn't know there were unicorns."

"They're the most magical ponies on the island," said Puck, "but they hardly ever come out, they're so shy. We learned all about them in Pony Magic School. They feed on magical golden apples that enhance their powers and give them amazing speed. They're even ruled by their own Unicorn Prince."

"I'd love to see a unicorn," said Holly, wistfully. "Are we allowed into the Enchanted Wood? Have you ever seen one?" she asked eagerly.

"Never," Puck replied. "You have to get special permission to go into the wood. I've never had any reason to go there, but maybe it would be different if I took you. It would be amazing!"

As they tucked into their picnic, Holly

forgot about the unicorns, enjoying the delicious food Bluebell had made for them. She popped rainbow drops into her mouth, where they fizzled and tickled her tongue, and sipped on honeydew juice, which glinted like liquid gold in the sun.

Then suddenly, from the other side of the meadow, came a desperate shout.

"Please!" called the voice. "What are you doing? Stop!"

"What's that?" cried Holly, the panic-stricken voice making her shiver. "What's happening?"

Chapter Two

Holly and Puck sprang up. They could see a group of ponies over by the woods. Then they heard another cry.

"Help me!"

"Quick! Onto my back!" Puck called, and Holly leaped on, wrapping her arms around him as he galloped across the meadow.

"It's a unicorn!" cried Holly, catching sight

of a small silvery-white pony with a gleaming horn, who looked about the same age as Puck. Even from a distance, Holly could see she was in trouble. Three large dark ponies had crowded around her, and they were now locked in some kind of struggle.

"Help!" the unicorn cried again. "Somebody stop them!"

"We're coming," Holly called back, as Puck strained forwards, desperately trying to cover the ground as fast as he could.

As they drew closer, Holly felt a jolt of fear as she recognized the other ponies. "It's Shadow," she said. "And Storm and Ravenstar. What are they doing?"

But before they could reach them, the big dark ponies took to the skies, swiftly disappearing over the treetops of the Enchanted Wood.

Puck made as if to fly after them, but Holly stopped him gently. "We'll never catch up with Shadow now," she said. "We must help the unicorn." She slipped off Puck's back and walked closer to the trembling creature. "Are you okay?" she asked Holly.

"How dare they!" the unicorn replied, stamping the ground, and Holly quickly realized she was trembling with rage, not fear. Puck looked at the unicorn with respect, while Holly stood mesmerized by her beauty. She had a gleaming silver coat, soft feathery wings and a horn that glistened like an ocean pearl.

"What's your name?" asked Holly softly.

"Willow," the unicorn replied.

"I'm Puck, and this is my friend, Holly," said Puck, quickly introducing them. "Please, tell us what happened."

The unicorn shook her silvery mane, as if trying to gather her thoughts. "I was

exploring the edge of the Enchanted Wood," she began, "when a dark fairy pony with huge wings came bursting through the trees. He said he'd found a baby unicorn just outside, in the meadow. He asked me to help guide the baby back into the wood, as she seemed scared of him. But as soon as we left the wood, I realized it was a trap. There was no baby unicorn!"

"That's just like Shadow," Puck muttered beneath his breath.

"Two more fairy ponies appeared," the unicorn went on. "They held onto my wings so I couldn't move, while the first pony stole a feather from my wing and a hair from my tail. Then they all flew off together."

"That sounds terrible!" said Holly. "Those ponies you met are very dangerous," she went on. "Their names are Shadow, Storm and Ravenstar. They're plotting to take over Pony Island."

Willow gasped as Holly said their names. "I've heard of them," she said. "There's been talk in the Enchanted Wood about Shadow and his wicked plots against the Pony Queen."

"We must find the Pony Queen right away," said Puck, turning to Holly. "This is urgent. She should know we saw Shadow."

"Wait!" cried Willow. "I don't know if there's time. I heard Shadow tell Storm and Ravenstar to follow him to the Unicorn Palace – I think they're after the Unicorn

Prince! Haven't you heard the legend?"

"What legend?" asked Puck.

"We're taught this in school," said Willow. "Listen...

If you wish to turn into a unicorn
With magical powers and a gleaming horn,
Take a hair from a tail and a feather from a wing
Then bind them together with silver string
From the royal crown take a leaf or two
Then say these words, let them ring true...
Make me into a unicorn, make me strong and wise,
Give me the power I crave to rule over the skies."

"Don't you see?" Willow finished. "If Shadow gets a leaf from the Prince's crown, he'll be able to turn himself into a unicorn. Then he'll be powerful enough to take over Pony Island."

"We have to stop him!" cried Holly. "We must warn the Unicorn Prince."

"Follow me," said Willow. "I'll show you the way to his palace."

She fluttered her feathery wings and soared into the sky. Holly leaped onto Puck's back and they rose into the air, Puck flying as fast as he could to keep up with Willow. Holly could only hold on tightly as they swept over the Enchanted Wood, desperate to reach the Prince before it was too late.

Chapter Three

Puck's glossy wings moved in smooth, strong beats, his hoofs clipping the treetops as they followed in Willow's wake. Holly noticed the unicorn's effortless speed as she zoomed ahead of them, her wings slicing through the air. Then suddenly, without warning, she dived down into a dense cluster of trees. Puck dropped down after her, and the next moment

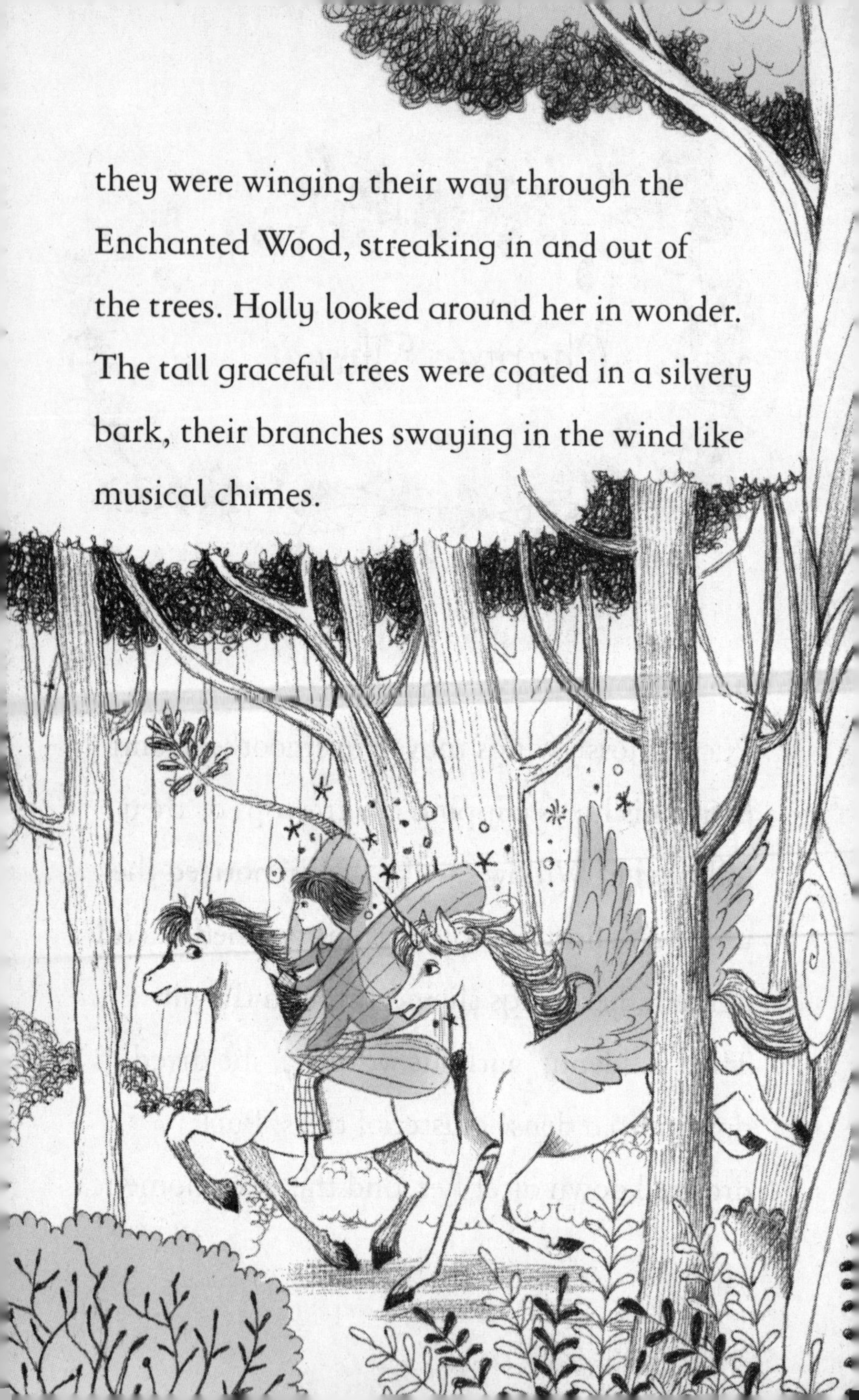

they were winging their way through the Enchanted Wood, streaking in and out of the trees. Holly looked around her in wonder. The tall graceful trees were coated in a silvery bark, their branches swaying in the wind like musical chimes.

Ahead, Holly saw Willow was heading for a small clearing. On one side of it, the way was blocked by a mass of tangled vines.

"We're here," whispered Willow, as Puck landed beside her in the clearing. "This is the entrance to the Unicorn Palace. I haven't been here for a while but I'm sure this is it."

"Where is the palace?" asked Holly, looking about in confusion.

Willow smiled. "Right in front of you," she said. "Watch!"

Willow began trotting up to the wall of knotted vines. As she reached them, they magically untangled, revealing a set of sparkling golden gates.

"Wow!" said Puck, following Willow. "I'd never have guessed the palace was here."

The gates opened to reveal a walkway lined with bushes and Holly gasped as she saw the white marble palace, surrounded by lush gardens. Puck, Holly and Willow began to approach as quietly as they could, glancing around for any sign of Shadow. But before they could reach the imposing doorway, there was a flurry of feathers and a flock of exotic birds swooped down from the trees. They surrounded Puck and Willow, frantically flapping their wings, making it hard for the ponies to move.

"Hey! What are you doing?" cried Willow, stepping back as the birds darted this way and that.

The birds chattered excitedly, their dazzling plumage making them flash like

jewels in the sunlight.

"Stop it! Let us through," said Willow huffily. "We need to help the Unicorn Prince."

But the birds' chatter only grew more excited and, chirping frantically, they swept around the ponies, as if they were trying to lead them away from the path.

"I think they're trying to tell us something," said Puck, looking curiously at the birds.

The birds seemed to nod as if in agreement, and Holly felt as if they were beckoning to her, trying to attract her attention. She slipped off Puck's back and followed their flight as they sped away from the path. The birds came to rest on the bough of a tree and, looking down, Holly spotted a trail of rose

petals, leading away
from the palace and
deep into the gardens.

"Look!" Holly cried. "I think they want us to follow this trail."

As Puck and Willow came galloping over, one of the biggest birds flew down from the tree until he was hovering just in front of Holly. Looking up, Holly realized he was holding a small scroll in his beak. She took it from him as gently as she could and unfurled it. With Puck and Willow glancing over her shoulders, they read the scroll:

To His Royal Highness,
the Unicorn Prince

From, Her Majesty,
the Pony Queen

I have sent you a magical gift
as a token of our friendship.
Follow the rose-petal trail to
find your present...

"Look, it's a letter from the Pony Queen," said Willow.

Puck was still staring at the silver hoof

mark at the bottom of the scroll. "No, it's not!" he cried. "That's not from the Pony Queen. Whenever she leaves her mark, her hoof print is surrounded by golden sparkles. I've seen her letters to my mum and the other Spell-Keepers. This looks like a fake!"

At Puck's words, the birds chirruped again and then began following the rose-petal trail, looking back as if to ask Holly and the ponies to follow them.

"We need to find out where the trail leads," said Puck. "It could mean danger for the Unicorn Prince."

Nodding in agreement, Holly climbed onto Puck's back and they set off again with Willow, this time following the rose petals between the trees. The trail twisted this way and that, until it led into a maze of high hedges set so close together that their tops almost blocked out the sun. As Puck, Holly and Willow entered the maze, the birds dropped back until they were alone, treading softly down the petal-strewn paths.

"What's this?" asked Holly, as she peered down at a trail of large hoof prints stretching in front of them, which had left the petals trampled into the ground.

"It looks like Shadow's been here already," said Puck anxiously. "Let's pick up the pace."

The deeper they went into the maze, the darker it became. Then the trail came to a sudden stop. Cautiously, Puck and Holly peered around the next corner, Willow craning her neck behind them. There, in the very heart of the maze, stood a beautiful rose bower, with velvety roses cascading down a waterfall of glossy leaves.

But as Holly looked closer, she spied the sharp thorns of the roses' twisting stems and realized the bower was no more than an exquisite cage. Trapped inside, his head tossed back with pride, stood the Unicorn Prince. Surrounding him, their expressions smug and gloating, were Shadow, Storm and Ravenstar.

"Oh no!" whispered Holly. "We're too late!"

Chapter Four

Shadow was standing close to the thorny branches of the bower, taunting the Prince. "You'll never get out," he said with a laugh. "And now you're just where I want you. I can't believe how easily you fell for my trap."

From their hiding place, Holly, Puck and Willow watched in dismay as the Unicorn Prince struggled against the bars of his cage, casting desperate spells with his horn, only to have them rebound off the branches of the enchanted bower.

Despite her fear, Holly felt dazzled by the Unicorn Prince's beauty. His hoofs sparkled with silver dust, his feathered wings shone brilliantly, and on his head sat a crown of glimmering, golden leaves.

Shadow's next words sliced through the air. "There's nothing you can do," he boasted. "I have a golden leaf from your crown – the last ingredient I need for my spell! Now you can watch me become a unicorn."

As he spoke, Shadow laid out the strand of hair from Willow's tail and the feather from her wing.

"Look!" whispered Willow. "He's tying them with silver string – just like the legend says."

"You cannot take on a unicorn's powers," said the Unicorn Prince, watching Shadow closely. "You lack the wisdom and the strength to control them."

"Oh really? Well, that's a risk I'm willing to take!" snarled Shadow, and he bowed his head and began to chant a spell.

"*A hair from a unicorn's tail, a feather*
from a unicorn's wing,
Rise before me in the air, bound with a silver string.
From the royal crown, a golden leaf,
sparkling in the sun,
Mix together in the air, my spell is nearly done.
Make me into a unicorn, make me strong and wise,
Give me the power I crave, to rule over the skies."

On his last words, there was a blinding flash of light. Holly, Puck and Willow stumbled back, shielding their eyes from the glare. When they looked again, Shadow stood before them, a gleaming twisted horn on his head.

“No!” cried the Unicorn Prince, pounding the ground with his hoofs.

Shadow turned his head, admiring his new horn. “Now to test my unicorn powers,” he said, and he lowered his horn and aimed

it at the rose bower. A lightning bolt of sparks shot out of his horn and the next moment all the rose petals fell to the ground, burning with black flames. The rose bower stayed standing, but its branches were charred and its leaves were blackened and scorched.

Shadow laughed triumphantly. "I have truly gained a unicorn's powers. And now the time has come for me to overthrow the Pony Queen. I've already sent a letter to her, inviting her to your palace. She thinks she's coming to meet you – but it'll be me she finds."

"How dare you—" began the Unicorn Prince.

Shadow interrupted him with a snap. "You're in no position to question my authority now," he said. "When the Pony

Queen arrives, she won't stand a chance against us. Then I can rule Pony Island in her place!"

Shadow beat his glittering wings and, as Holly looked on in anguish, he took to the skies with Storm and Ravenstar, heading for the Unicorn Palace.

Chapter Five

As Shadow and his henchmen disappeared into the distance, Willow rushed over to the Unicorn Prince, tears streaming down her face. "I'm so sorry," she said. "We were too late to warn you. Shadow stole a feather from my wing and a hair from my tail, but when we got here we didn't know how to stop him…"

"It's not your fault," said the Unicorn

Prince, his voice deep and calm, although his eyes were still flooded with anger. "There's nothing you could have done to stop Shadow. And I'm afraid there's nothing you can do to free me now. The magic of the bower is too strong for you."

Up close, Holly could see the Prince's horn gleamed like a pearl, while his elegant crown of golden leaves sparkled in the dappled forest light. Everything about him seemed pure and regal – the very opposite of Shadow. "There must be something we can do!" she cried, unable to bear the thought that Shadow had won.

"This is Holly and her friend Puck," Willow explained quickly. "They came to my aid when Shadow tricked me."

"You are the first child ever to enter the Enchanted Wood," said the Unicorn Prince, gazing at Holly. "I believe there may be something you can do to help us stop Shadow."

"Please, tell me what it is," said Holly.

"There's a very dangerous plant that can take away a pony's, or a unicorn's magic for ever," the Unicorn Prince explained. "It is called Stinkwort and it grows in a secret place in the palace gardens, tucked away behind the golden orchard. You'll find it in a dark and shady corner, just beyond the crooked tree."

A look of terror crossed Willow's face. "Stinkwort?" she whispered. "But if we touch it, won't it take away our magic powers too?"

"It could," replied the Unicorn Prince.

"That's why Holly is the only one who can touch it. Come here, Holly," he went on, beckoning her towards him. "You will need to open the enchanted gates that protect the Stinkwort."

Holly bent closer as the Unicorn Prince whispered a secret spell in her ear. "Can you remember that?" he asked.

Holly nodded nervously, but she couldn't help feeling proud of her mission.

"Don't let the others touch it," the Unicorn Prince went on, "in case it harms them. To remove Shadow's powers, you must squeeze the Stinkwort's sap over his horn. Now go, as quickly as you can. And good luck."

Holly felt the weight of what they were doing on her shoulders. Shadow was more powerful than he had ever been before. She knew that trying to stop him was a dangerous task.

Together, Holly, Puck and Willow hurried back through the maze, following the trail of petals, pale and wilting where they had been trodden into the soft earth.

"This way to the orchard," said Willow, galloping out of the maze and across the palace gardens.

Holly climbed onto Puck's back and they cantered after her, Holly glancing anxiously from side to side for any sign of Shadow or his henchmen.

As they raced to the Stinkwort, Holly caught tantalizing glimpses of the beautiful gardens. They were bursting with luscious exotic flowers, their heady scents hanging heavy in the summer air. Fountains splashed sparkling water into deep, clear pools filled with silvery fish. Holly was amazed to see the palace lawn was also dotted with statues of

unicorns, so lifelike that she expected them to take to the air at any moment.

"They're amazing," Holly said to Puck, looking at one statue kneeling on the grass beneath a tree, seemingly gazing up at the sky. She could even see the details of the feathers on the smooth, stone wings.

At last they came to the orchard, where the ancient boughs of the apple trees were weighed down with golden fruit. Long grass grew between the trees, thick with wild flowers. Holly noticed more statues as they passed – a unicorn with braids in her mane and tail, carrying a basket of apples, another with a gardening fork between his teeth.

"It feels so still here," Holly began. "As if the statues are watching us, or waiting for something..." She stopped as she heard a faint cry from Willow, and turned to look at her.

Willow was standing in front of a statue of a unicorn rearing up on his hind legs, his eyes blazing. Around his hoofs, fluttering in the breeze, was a strip of fabric, emblazoned with the Prince's crown of leaves. "They're not statues," she gasped. "I know this unicorn – he's one of the palace guards. That's his sash at his feet. All these statues... They're unicorns...turned to stone!"

Chapter Six

Willow turned to look at Puck and Holly, an expression of pure terror on her face. "This must be Shadow's work. Just imagine what would happen if Shadow did rule Pony Island."

"We must stop him," said Holly, fear filling her with determination. "Come on – let's find the Stinkwort."

She slid from Puck's back and ran through the rest of the orchard, Puck and Willow behind her, unable to tear their eyes from the eerie statues. At last they came to an ancient apple tree, its trunk growing at a strange, crooked angle from the ground. Beyond it lay a pair of iron gates, almost hidden in the orchard wall beneath layers of ivy. "This must be it," said Holly, and she bent down to the keyhole and whispered the words of the spell:

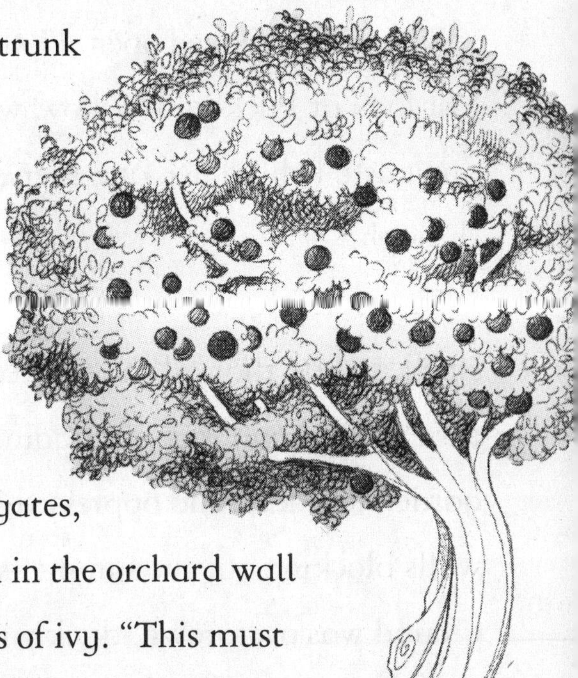

The gates creaked open. Holly took one last look at Puck and Willow, waiting anxiously behind her, and then slipped through.

Immediately, she was hit by a terrible smell, so bad that all she wanted to do was turn around and race out again. The tiny garden felt dark and oppressive, its high stone walls blocking out the summer sun. The ground was overgrown, thick with tangled thorns and weeds, but it was easy to find the Stinkwort. *It really lives up to its name,* thought Holly. The Stinkwort reeked. It grew in messy clumps between the weeds, with spiky leaves and dark, bruised flowers. Hurriedly, before the smell overpowered her, Holly picked as much as she could and stuffed it in her pocket.

Then she raced outside again, to the sweet, fresh air of the orchard, and the heavy iron doors clanged shut behind her.

"You stink!" said Puck, smiling at her, clearly relieved that she was safely out of the garden. "I'm not sure I'm going to let you ride on my back smelling like that."

Willow looked at her anxiously. "Have you got it safely hidden away?" she asked.

"Yes," Holly promised. "It's in my pocket. I won't let it touch you. And now, I suppose we should find Shadow," she finished nervously.

Puck sensed her nerves and paused for a

moment. He glanced from Willow to the golden apples, hanging from the boughs of the trees. "Willow," he said thoughtfully, "do you think if I ate one of your magic apples, I'd gain unicorn powers?"

"Yes!" said Willow. "That's a brilliant idea! I don't know how long the apple's powers would last though. Why don't you take one and eat it just before we get to the palace?"

Puck quickly picked an apple and passed it to Holly, who dropped it into her other pocket. "Now I feel ready to face Shadow," he said.

Holly breathed a sigh of relief. She felt a little more confident, knowing that Puck would have extra powers. "Okay," she said, clambering onto his back. "Let's go!"

They galloped back through the gardens to

the palace and crept in through a side entrance. As quietly as they could, they followed the palace's winding corridors, the ponies' ears pricked as they listened for any sign of Shadow and his henchmen.

As they turned a corner, Willow's face looked grim. "Another statue," she whispered, as they passed a stone unicorn, its head bowed as if trying to shield itself from Shadow's spell. "We're definitely on the right track."

The palace was eerily silent as they passed statue after statue of unicorn servants and palace guards, each face frozen in fear or anger. Holly couldn't help a flutter of nerves in her stomach – would she be able to get the Stinkwort onto Shadow in time, or would they too be turned to stone?

"Listen!" said Willow suddenly. "I think I can hear something."

The three of them followed the sound of voices until they came to a great hall – a vast airy room lined with marble columns and topped with a lofty dome. Swooping above them on his powerful wings was Shadow, watched by Storm and Ravenstar.

"These unicorn powers are amazing!" Shadow cried. He swished his head and Holly gasped to see a freezing spell strike one of the columns, turning it to ice.

"How can we stop him?" whispered Willow. "Look how powerful he is."

"We have to try," said Puck. "The Pony Queen could be here any moment."

"Puck's right," Holly agreed. "We have no choice. It's up to us now. We can't let Shadow take over Pony Island."

Chapter Seven

Holly took a deep breath. "We need a plan," she whispered. "Willow, do you think you can distract Shadow, so that Puck and I can get in close with the Stinkwort?"

Willow nodded, her eyes fixed on Shadow. "Puck, now's the time to eat your golden apple."

Holly passed the apple to Puck, who ate it

as quickly as he could. Immediately, he was surrounded by a burst of sparkles. His whole body began to quiver, as if filled with energy.

"Wow!" he said. "I feel amazing. Quick, Holly, jump on my back! Let's go!"

Holly leaped onto Puck's back and reached for the Stinkwort in her pocket, her heart hammering.

Willow zoomed out in front of them, flying fast and low, as if aiming for one of the open

windows. “You again!” cried Shadow, as she shot past him. “The helpful little unicorn. What are you doing here? I think you need to be taught a lesson.”

He lowered his horn to blast a spell at her, but at the last moment Willow darted away, flying towards the great oak doors on the other side of the hall. As Shadow began to

pursue her, Puck didn't waste a moment. He slipped out from their hiding place and headed straight for Shadow, pounding the air with his wings. Holly pulled out the Stinkwort, ready to squeeze the sap over his horn – but fiery sparks were already flying from Shadow's horn. There was a single cry from Willow, then silence. Holly and Puck could only gaze in horror as they saw her turned to stone.

"Behind you!" cried Storm, his attention caught by Puck and Holly. He and Ravenstar shot into the air, but Shadow only laughed. "Leave these two to me," he said.

In an instant, Shadow's horn was pointing their way. Puck veered to the side, just in time, as a firebolt came shooting through the air. Shadow cast another and another, forcing Puck to zigzag madly around the room. Out of the corner of her eye, Holly could see Storm and Ravenstar

quickly flying around the doors and windows, casting spells to slam them shut.

"They're trapping us," she realized with a clutch of fear.

Holly could feel Puck was growing tired. "We've got to strike now," she whispered in his ear. "Head straight for Shadow. It's our only chance."

"Okay," Puck agreed, taking a deep breath. He put his head down and raced through the air like a speeding arrow, aiming for Shadow's horn. Holly stretched out her hand with the Stinkwort, carefully keeping it away from Puck, her fingers ready to squeeze out its powerful sap.

Shadow looked up, startled. For a moment he seemed confused, then he shot out another firebolt. "Watch out!" cried Holly, as the stream of fire headed straight for them.

Puck didn't swerve from his course, until Holly was sure they were going to be struck down, but at the last moment he swooped to the side so the firebolt streaked past them. Puck kept heading straight for Shadow, and Holly grabbed her chance. She squeezed the Stinkwort between her trembling fingers and watched with relief as she saw its slimy sap ooze out, dripping then clinging onto Shadow's gleaming horn.

There was a sizzling sound followed by a loud bang that sent Puck and Holly spinning backwards. Holly just managed to cling onto Puck's mane as they were whooshed through the air. When she looked up again she gave a cry of joy. "Look, Puck! Shadow's horn has disappeared!"

As Puck came to rest on the ground, Holly smiled with relief. She leaned down and hugged him, resting her head on his silky-soft mane. He was panting with exhaustion and Holly could see his magical glow had grown fainter as the apple's magic powers began to fade away. "We did it just in time," she said.

But as she glanced up at Shadow, Holly realized the battle wasn't over yet. He was seething, his dark eyes glittering with silent fury.

"What have you done?" he snarled, dropping down on the other side of the hall. He tried sending another firebolt at them, but nothing happened. He reared up, stamping his hoofs on the marble floor, tossing his mane wildly.

"You may have stolen away my unicorn powers, but you're not going to get away with this," he said. "Storm! Ravenstar! Let's get them!"

Chapter Eight

"You don't stand a chance against us!" snarled Shadow, as the three dark ponies advanced menacingly.

Puck and Holly were trapped against the wall of the great hall. Suddenly there was a loud crashing sound, followed by a burst of light. The doors flew open and the Pony Queen galloped in, flanked by the Unicorn

Prince and the palace guards.

"Your wicked unicorn spells are broken," said the Unicorn Prince. "All the statues are coming back to life."

Shadow, Storm and Ravenstar exchanged glances. "We're outnumbered," said Shadow, through gritted teeth. "It's time to go."

Ravenstar uttered a spell beneath his breath and the next moment the room was filled with black smoke.

The Pony Queen and the Unicorn Prince darted forwards, but it was impossible to see anything. By the time the smoke had cleared, Shadow and his henchmen had gone.

"There they are!" cried Holly. One of the windows was now wide open, and beyond it, Holly could see three black shapes soaring through the sky.

"After them!" cried the Unicorn Prince, and the palace guards streaked through the window, their expressions grim and determined.

In the corner of the great hall, Holly saw Willow was finally coming back to life. She rushed over to her, just as the little unicorn shakily stood up.

"Did it work?" asked Willow. "Did we stop Shadow?"

"Yes," said the Unicorn Prince. "I owe you three a huge debt of gratitude." He turned to the Pony Queen. "It is thanks to Puck, Holly and Willow that Shadow has not done more damage today. They found me trapped in the enchanted bower, gathered the Stinkwort and bravely came to the palace to rid Shadow of his unicorn powers. Without them, who knows what might have happened when you arrived."

The Pony Queen looked at Puck and Holly, her eyes shining with pride. "Well done," she said quietly, in her musical voice. "And my thanks to you too, Willow. You have all acted courageously today."

"And now," said the Unicorn Prince, "I would like to reward you for your bravery. Name your prize."

Puck didn't think for long. "I'm starving!" he said. "You see, Holly and I never got to finish our picnic this morning..."

The Unicorn Prince laughed. "Then a picnic it shall be. Come with me to the palace gardens. But first, I'd better tidy this place up." He gave a quick look around the great hall, taking in the damage that Shadow had done, then cast a spell.

"Great hall, shining white,
Rid yourself of Shadow's blight.
Return now to your former glory
It's time to tell a different story."

As they all headed out into the garden, Holly glanced back to see the Unicorn

Prince's magic at work. Black marks where firebolts had struck the floor vanished in an instant and the frozen columns returned to shining marble, leaving no trace of Shadow's presence.

"Now," the Unicorn Prince declared, as they stood in the sunlit garden, "it's time for a feast."

At his words, the dazzling birds who had helped them earlier appeared in the sky, carrying woven baskets. They fluttered down, chirruping excitedly, laying their gifts on the ground. Holly saw the baskets were filled with delicious food – bunches of golden grapes, tiny cakes, each decorated with a sparkling silver hoof mark, peaches and star fruit, rainbow bonbons and bottles of sparkling golden apple juice.

"It looks AMAZING!" said Puck, as he took it all in. "This was definitely worth waiting for."

Holly looked around in wonder. She couldn't believe she was in such a beautiful spot. The Pony Queen and the Unicorn Prince talked together, while Puck and Willow tucked into the picnic.

Beyond them, other unicorns were arriving for the feast, flying through the palace gardens on their graceful feathered wings.

Holly sat back, a ripe warm peach in one hand, a mouth-watering cake in the other, and watched the water splashing from the fountains into the sparkling pools. The birds had started to sing, creating a musical backdrop of tinkling notes that rose and fell like gentle waves.

Then, from the other end of the garden came a Spell-Keeper, who raced towards the Pony Queen. "Your Majesty," he said, his voice breathless from flying. "The others are still searching for Shadow, but I came to tell you there's no sign of him. It's as if he's disappeared."

"We must keep searching," replied the Pony Queen. "And we must continue to be on our guard. But we have triumphed over Shadow today, and we will do so again."

"And you'll always have our help, too," added the Unicorn Prince. "But that is enough of Shadow for today." He looked at Puck and Holly and smiled. "In return for your help, I am granting you permission to enter the Enchanted Wood whenever you desire. You will always be welcome here – as our special guests."

"Wow!" said Puck, grinning over at Holly. "I mean, thank you, Your Majesty."

"We can come here whenever we want!" Holly whispered, in a daze of happiness. "Pony Island just keeps getting better and better. I can't wait to find out what amazing magical adventures we'll have next!"

Midnight Escape

ISBN: 9781409506287

Holly is staying with her Great-Aunt May when she discovers a tiny pony with shimmering wings. At first she thinks she must be dreaming...until two fairy ponies visit her with an urgent mission.

Magic Necklace

ISBN: 9781409506294

Holly and her friend Puck are visiting the Pony Queen when a magical necklace is stolen from the palace. Can Puck and Holly help track it down before the thief uses its magic?

Rainbow Races

ISBN: 9781409506300

Holly can't wait to watch her friend Puck compete in the Rainbow Races. But when an enchanted storm is unleashed over Pony Island, ruining the races, the home of the fairy ponies is threatened with darkness for ever...

Pony Princess

ISBN: 9781409506379

When the Fairy Pony Princess comes to visit, Puck and Holly are given the all-important job of looking after her. But then their royal guest goes missing. Can Puck and Holly find her again?

Unicorn Prince

ISBN: 9781409506362

Holly and Puck uncover a wicked plot to take over Pony Island. To save the day, they must venture into the Enchanted Wood, home of the mysterious unicorns…

Enchanted Mirror

ISBN: 9781409506386

Pony Island is in danger. The ponies are losing their magic and the Pony Queen's powers are under threat. Can Holly and Puck uncover the mystery of the missing magic, before it's too late?

Edited by Stephanie King and Becky Walker

Designed by Brenda Cole

Additional design by Elisabetta Barbazza

Reading consultant: Alison Kelly,
University of Roehampton

First published in 2014 by Usborne Publishing Ltd.,
Usborne House, 83-85 Saffron Hill, London EC1N 8RT, England.
www.usborne.com

Cover and inside illustrations by Barbara Bongini

A CIP catalogue record for this book is available from the British Library.